The Little Stubborn Boy who became a Bishop

The Little Stubborn Boy who became a Bishop

Maureen Nwajiobi

THE LITTLE STUBBORN BOY WHO BECAME A BISHOP

iUniverse books may be ordered through booksellers or by contacting:

iUniverse
1663 Liberty Drive
Bloomington, IN 47403
www.iuniverse.com
844-349-9409

ISBN: 978-1-6632-3960-0 (sc)
ISBN: 978-1-6632-3961-7 (e)

Print information available on the last page.

iUniverse rev. date: 05/06/2022

To the Daughters of Mary
Mother of Mercy (DMMM)

To my family and in loving memory of my dear parents,
Mr. and Mrs. Michael Nwajiobi

Contents

Preface

Little Edward and the Church is a work of fiction combined with practical life lessons. When I was growing up, I found myself in a devout Catholic home. Going to Church with my parents, siblings and my experiences in the Church inspired me to write this book. Writing this book, most of my inspiration for this book came to me while praying in the Chapel. The most interesting thing was that the thoughts which kept coming and flowing were connected to the reality that I have observed seeing little children struggling with their parents in the Church and I have also observed these kids gazing and admiring things that caught their attention in the Church. I imagined what goes on in their young mind. Any attractive object especially the decorations and things that happen in the surroundings of the Church can hold their attention span and at the same time the experience can help them all through life. The reality of life shows from the fact that we learn a lot from what happens around us. It is also particularly important to emphasize that we learn a lot from the foundation given to us and the things we learn when we were young. It is my intention to draw the attention of Church goers to the things happening in the Church and the surrounding. It is also important to remind us of the importance of appreciating what we have.

In this book, little Edward who did not want to go to Church because it was boring, used the activities in the Church to capture and entertain himself, in the end, he loved going to Church and later became important person in the Church. He also used his experience to help many people whose stories in this book will interest and capture your attention to the end.

I want to thank the members of my religious family, the Daughters of Mary Mother of Mercy for their encouragement and support. I wish to express my gratitude to Fr. Livinus Torty, MSP for his advice and support, and Fr. Martin J. Lott, OP for his valuable advice. I thank Mr. Tom Furmanczyk for proofreading the manuscript. I also thank the members of my natural family, the Nwajiobi family, especially my brother, Fr. Michael Jude Nwajiobi for his support. I remember my late parents, Mr. Michael, and Mrs. Catherine Nwajiobi.

Sr. Maureen Nwajiobi DMMM
Houston, Texas, November 2022

Introduction

Little Edward and the Church features a young boy who did not want to go to Church because it was boring to him. His major problem was that his parents did not allow him to play as he used to do when they visit other places. He tried to avoid going to Church but realized that he had no choice than to follow his parents to Church to avoid punishment. Edward was a curious child that likes to ask questions. He wanted clarifications in everything, and he learned a lot. His parents did not allow him to ask questions during Mass, neither did they allow him to play. He devised means to entertain himself to avoid boredom. He found a lot of interesting things going on in the Church during the Mass, like the music, the huge cross hanging in the Church and the altar servers. From admiring and watching the altar servers, he found out that he could join them, after becoming an altar server, he wanted to go to the Seminary, after completing his seminary studies, he accepted ordination and he became a priest. The interesting thing about the book was that what motivated Edward to avoid boredom in the Church developed into a virtue, a virtue that he shared with many people he encountered. Edward believed that if you do not like something or someone, discover something interesting in the thing or person, entertain yourself with it, love, appreciate it and you will gradually learn to love. He strongly believed that there is always something good and special about everyone. In this book, the stories of the people that he helped through his experiences are enriching, interesting and educational.

Chapter 1

I do not want to go to Church

One cold windy evening stood a 5-year-old Edward, it could easily be seen that Edward's parents were dragging Edward to the Church. His face was not pleasant, "I don't want to go to Church," he said. Edward categorically made it clear that he did not want to go inside the Church with them. As Edwards parents were arguing and battling with him, the Church bell rang, startling Edward. He wondered why they were ringing the bell. His parents Mr. Eddy and Mrs. Cathy Hilford explained to him that the bell is warning everyone that it is time to enter the Church for Mass. The Church was one of the ancient Churches in the city. Though the Church was old, it still looks magnificent because the priest in charge, staff and the Church parishioners constantly renovated and beautified it. The inside looked like you are already in heaven. They decorated the Church with pictures, and statues that keep you wondering about the beauty of God. The golden color and the combination of other colors made it look more beautiful. The outside of the Church was not as beautiful as the inside. Edward had earlier attended the Mass with his parents and concluded that he will not attend the Mass again. The experience was not enjoyable. He explained to his parents that the reason behind his decision was that the Church was boring. He pinpointed that there was no fun inside the church, more particularly his parents being staunch Catholic would not allow him to move around or play with his 3-year-old younger brother. Edward further said that the most annoying part was when his parents hit him on the lap to pay attention to the priest. This was unlike their visit to the beach or movie theatre room where his parents allowed him to play and have fun. No matter the preaching they gave to Edward, he did not want to change his mind about going to the Church. If Edward had the option to choose, he would have chosen not to follow his family to Church.

When it was clear to Edward that he cannot continue to fight his parents, he gave up. He remembered that there could be punishment for his actions. It became obvious to him that the only option left for him was to obey and follow his parents. He decided to find something that would fascinate him, something that can captivate his attention during the time spent in the Church. As they were walking inside the Church, he started admiring the drawings, architecture, paintings, and statues. He found them remarkably interesting to watch. He saw the altar servers and found them very fascinating, they are young kids like him. Wait a minute! What are they doing? Wondered Edward. He noticed that the altar servers were in line walking up in procession to the altar with hands joined together in their ceremonial uniform. They were walking in front of the priest. He noticed that they were young children and one of them might be as young as him. He liked the way they joined their hands like the angels in his book. He curiously watched and noticed that they were helping the priest. He found them interesting to watch.

During consecration, Edward was still wondering why his parents insisted that he must kneel with them, the bell rang, and he looked, it was one of the altar servers that rang the bell. He kneeled and watched with interest what will happen next. Simultaneously, everyone stood up singing. Edward liked the music and the choir. During the communion time, his parents told him to cross his hands so that the priest will bless him. He liked that the priest touched and seemed to pray for him. He liked how everyone lined up to receive Jesus which he cannot receive now until he learns everything about receiving him. He secretly admired those that receive Jesus, when he found out that even the younger children receive him. He wondered how Jesus can be as little as the white thing people receive in their mouth or in their hands. His parents received in their mouth. Edward has lots of questions to ask about this Jesus. He has questions about the reception of the communion, but his parents would not answer them during Mass. They wanted him to remain quiet and pay attention during the Mass. Even though his parents are making things difficult for him inside the Church, he has already discovered several things that can hold his attention. He remembered the altar servers and found what they were doing interesting at least they are not sitting still. They are busy up there; they can easily move around and help the priest. He thought about joining them, but he remembered that people will be watching him, and he was shy to endure that. He dismissed the thought. Without wasting time, everyone stood up, the priest prayed and blessed them, and he dismissed them. He discovered that they do not have to stay all day in the Church. He concluded that he will not have issues with his parents again about going to the Church.

When they got home, instead of waiting for his parents to call him and scold him or give him timeout, Edward decided to apologize for misbehaving in the Church. His parents were surprised at what he did. They told him to sit down quietly and listen to them. He obeyed and sat quietly, looking up to them like a prodigal son seeking forgiveness from his father. They explained the importance of Mass to him. They used the opportunity to answer his questions in the Church. They explained to Edward that God is almighty, and everyone should respect him. They explained that all those people in the Church gathered to adore and give thanks to God. While they were explaining to Edward, he asked his parents "if Jesus is almighty, why was he hanging on the cross, suffering?" Edward's parents were surprised at his question. Edward asked again, 'what did he do"?

Edwards parents explained to him that Jesus did not do anything wrong. He only came down to suffer, die and save us from our sins. Surprised, Edward asked his parents "You sin"? His mother almost tired of his over inquisitive son explained to him that we are all sinners. Jesus died to show us love because while we are sinners, he agreed to suffer and die for us, his mother continued. Edward's confused face showed that he did not fully understand and as a result, he still has numerous questions to ask. His mother prepared food and they all ate and watched TV.

Chapter 2

Family Setup

──────── ❧ ────────

Mr. Eddy and Mrs. Cathy Hilford met, fell in love, eventually Eddy proposed, and Cathy accepted. They planned to get married in the courthouse first, but Eddy's parents discouraged civil marriage. They said that it will be better to get married in the Church first. Cathy's parents are Catholics too, but they are not so committed or devoted like Eddy's parents. They believe that their children are responsible and can take responsibility for their decisions in life. They do not want to interfere or enforce their wishes on their children. The parents of the bride did not like their in-laws domineering attitude, however, when they realized that their daughter was madly in love with Eddy, they consented. They also realized that their in-laws meant well for their children. They learned how to say a couple of prayers from them.

Cathy's parents had witnessed their in-laws hurrying their conversation to avoid missing their family prayer time. They knew they do not say such prayers in their family. One day they visited their in-laws, it rained so bad that they decided to wait a little while for the rain to stop. Eddy's parents announced that it is time for their family prayers, they invited them to be part of the prayer. Cathy's parents do not have such prayerful tradition, but they have no choice than to join them. Eddy's parents prayed so long that they seemed to have forgotten that they still have visitors with them. Cathy's parents knew the Rosary prayer, but they cannot say it without a prayer guide. They are only Sunday Church goers. They even skip going to Church some Sundays to stay at home and relax. The few minutes prayer with their in-laws changed their life. They stepped up and started praying themselves in their family.

Cathy grew up in such family and now transitioned to Eddy's family prayer tradition. Cathy adapted easily to the tradition because she loves her husband and she later realized that prayer is nourishing to the soul. She joined her husband in their family prayer. She was happy that her own family was supportive of her new prayer life. Having listened to Eddy's parents' explanation about the priority of getting married in the Church, she willingly loved the idea. Knowing fully well that any spiritual journey she started with Eddy will benefit them and their children. She started their marriage preparations with Eddy, and they enjoyed the program. They learned a lot from it.

They got married in the Church shortly before the death of Eddy's parents. Eddy missed and often remembered his parents' spirituality as staunch Catholics, he appreciated how they encouraged Cathy and himself to get married in the Church. He remembered how they convinced and modelled to them that by getting married in the Church, the couple receives God's blessing from God. Eddy and Cathy just came back from their honeymoon when Eddy's mother died, and his father could not bear it because they loved each other so much, he died of heart attack. Eddy vowed to keep to his promise of bringing their unborn babies closer to God and to continue to participate actively in the Church. He vividly understood Edward when he stated that he did not want to participate in the Church. He remembered doing the same thing when he was Edward's age. He remembered that even though he did not like going to Church with his parents, he realized that with time he became inexplicably drawn to the Church that he now views going to Church as an occasion to practice his faith and not as mere obligation.

Taking Edward along with him to Church is part of his promises to his parents to raise his children in the fear of the Lord Jesus. He is convinced that Edward will understand the importance of Mass when he grows up. He wondered the kind of child Edward will become, he is curious and intelligent. Aside from going to the Church, Edward's father continued their family tradition of saying their Rosary before they go to sleep in the evening. He would want the tradition to continue. Edward finds family prayer boring, but he is vibrant at watching to see who will sleep off so that he can tell on them. As time progresses, he is 9-year-old now. He learned how to say the prayers fluently and likes to lead. Edward slept sometimes during their family prayers but most times he stayed awake.

Edward was not the only child of Eddy and Cathy. After Edward, they have two more children, a boy, and a girl. The other two are not as inquisitive as Edward, they are not as extroverted either. Edward has lots of questions to ask at any given time. He learned so fast from asking many questions. Even his teachers at school are tired of his questions. Some of his questions surprise both his parents and his teachers. Edward likes his siblings. He cares about them, and they are happy to play with him. It was easier for Edward's siblings to learn how to stay calm in the Church because they learned from him. He gestures at them to keep quiet when they want to play. While the youngest child leans on his mother, the boy wants to stay close to Edward.

Edward used his siblings as his students and practiced teaching and asking them questions. Edward's younger brother liked to ask Edward questions instead of their parents, this was because Edward was ever ready to teach them. He once asked Edward what Jesus had done for him to be hanging on the cross in pain. Edward gave him the response that came from her mother when he asked the same question years back. He told his brother that Jesus did nothing wrong, he is God, but he became human to suffer, die and save us from our sins. The more Edward learns about God, the more he loves him and wants to serve him. Some Sundays, when they come back from the Church, he likes to play the role of a priest and he position his siblings as his altar servers.

Edward stopped disagreeing with his parents about going to the Church. He willingly attends the Church with them. The Church is no longer a boring but interesting place. A lot of things made Edward look forward to coming to the Church, the most interesting was the Altar servers. Initially, it bothered him that if he became one of the altar servers, people might be looking at him but since he started practicing with his siblings, he gained confidence. He willingly wanted to serve God and the priest at the altar. Initially, he looked around in the Church to find something that can get rid of his boredom, having found music and altar servers interesting, he admired it and now, he wants to be part of it. He likes the Church now.

Chapter 3

I want to serve in the Church

————— ❦ —————

Edward's approach about the Church has completely changed and evolved. He was excited one Sunday, when the parish children were getting ready to receive the sacrament of the Holy Eucharist, the parish priest spoke to the children in the first communion class, he explained the privileges of receiving the Sacrament. The priest asked few questions which Edward easily answered without hesitation. Edward was so happy the day he received the sacrament of the Holy Eucharist. Something seemed to have happened. He felt so joyous that at last he can now receive the body of Christ. He was also happy that he can now join the altar servers. He earlier wanted to join, and they explained to him that he can only join when he has received the Holy Eucharist.

Edward's joy knows no bound as he looks forward to Sunday Mass on Sundays and some weekdays. He repeatedly declares his interest in joining the altar servers. His parents spoke with the leader of the altar servers. He explained to them that candidates that want to join must receive their first Holy Communion, they should know how to make sign of the cross and genuflect, dress appropriately, they should arrive early before Mass begins, they should be able to maintain silence at the altar during Mass. They should be ready to have their hands joined.

Eddy and Cathy explained to the leader that their son had received the Holy Communion and that he is ready to abide by the rules. They further explained that their son is willing to serve God and assist the priest at the altar. Edward's heart was racing with uncertainty, fear, and hope that something positive may come out of this conversation. He stood like an angel with hands joined to impress the leader. The leader looked at him intently and asked him his name. Edward introduced himself with utter humility. The leader gave him high five and told him that he is free to join the group. He gave Eddy and Cathy a form they needed to fill and sign. He gave them another form with detailed explanation of the time for their practice and their rules and regulations. Edward was incredibly happy. He happily mumbled 'thank you Sir' to the leader.

The leader did not schedule Edward immediately to give him ample time to watch and practice. When he eventually scheduled him to serve, Edward was confident that he will serve without mistakes. The Sunday he served was a remarkable day for him. He was happy that he was able to serve this God that humbled himself to become human, suffered and died for us. He was happy because he was able to stand at the altar and assist the priest. However, he was disappointed that he made minor mistakes despite the practice he made in the Church and at home. He was more annoyed at the two altar servers who giggled and silently laughed at his mistakes.

He thought about reporting the two altar servers that laughed at his minor mistakes to the leader but changed his mind when their leader patted him on his back and congratulated him. He advised him to be calm and watchful of what other altar servers do whenever he is at the altar. Edward felt much better, he liked the leader for praising him and at the same time advised him. He ignored the attitude of the two altar servers that laughed at him. He decided to adhere to the advice of their leader and be more focused at the altar.

The subsequent Sundays that they scheduled Edward to serve were amazing. He served excellently well with zeal and passion. The leader noticed Edwards rapt enthusiasm and praised again. It propelled him to serve better and better. Eddy, Cathy, and Cathy's parents were so proud of him. They noticed his dedication and reverence to God while at the altar. Edward noticed that something he cannot explain happens to him whenever he revers and serves God at the altar. He felt that he belonged to the altar even though he cannot explain it. He longed, yearned, and waited for them to schedule him to serve. He looked forward to it. Edwards closeness to God even affected his devotion to God during their normal family prayer at home. He stayed awake all the time during prayers and he advised his siblings to stay focused during prayers.

Edward's dedication made his parents happy. He actively listened and participated during Mass when they did not schedule him to serve as altar server at the altar. He tried to explain things to his brother and sister. However, his parents did not allow him to talk during the Mass. He understood that it is important to accord God respect by keeping quiet, however, he was so enthusiastic about teaching the brother and sister so that they can learn. Surprisingly, his siblings do not ask too many questions like he does. Edward's behaviour and maturity in the Church surprises his parents. They remember when they were arguing with him to get into the Church. They are happy that he has changed, instead of seeing the Church as boring, he sees the Church as a vital space where he can pray and serve God as altar server.

An important development in Edward's life started as he continued to meditate on Jesus on the cross. To avoid boredom in the Church when he was younger, he used to watch Jesus on the crucifix, pity him and wished that he can remove the nails in his hands and legs and bring him down from the cross. Now Edward does not look at Jesus hanging on the cross to avoid boredom, he now worships, pities him, appreciates him, and wishes to reciprocate his love and sacrifice. As the day goes by, he loves Jesus increasingly and longs to serve and see him more often. Edward wanted his family to attend not only the Sunday Masses but regular weekday Masses.

Eddy and Cathy sparingly attend the weekday Masses with their children because of their work schedule but with recent development with the pleas for daily attendance of weekday Mass, they adjusted their work schedule to attend at least two or three weekday Masses during the week. Edward's devotion to God continues to increase. Eddy and Cathy were surprised at his attitude one Sunday morning when they informed their children that they cannot attend Mass because they are sick with flu. They wanted to avoid spreading the flu to other people in the Church since it is contagious. They were shocked when Edward started crying, as they were trying to console and make him understand, the other two joined Edward. When they could not bear it or stop them, Cathy decided to attend the Mass with them since her flu is not as serious as Eddy's flu.

When Eddy and Cathy were still dealing with Edward's new increasing devotion to God, Edward nurtured his interest to enter the Seminary School. Edward already had a deeper relationship with God but wanted to serve God more. During the Mass on a Sunday morning, their parish priest had praised two Seminarians that were on vacation and came back to their home parish. He praised them for giving their lives to God. He encouraged young people that want to serve God to join. He further declared that the Church needs more priests. He encouraged the people that have been praying for vocations to priesthood to intensify their prayers. Edward made up his mind to join the Seminary. It was not just because of what the parish priest said, he wanted to join because he was in love with God and wanted to serve him more in a unique way. He nurtured his interest to join the Seminary in his mind and prayed to God for guidance and support.

Chapter 4

I want to stay in the Seminary

The inquisitive nature of Edward made him learn a lot for his age. He was determined to make good grades in school to excel in his aspirations and dreams. His major focus and dream were to serve God as a priest. The more he practiced being a priest with his siblings, the more serious he becomes about being a priest. He could not summon the courage to mention it to his parents. He secretly admired priests. When he could not hide his feelings any longer, he confided in his brother who ran and told his parents in excitement that his big brother will become a priest. His parents felt that he was too young to take such decision. They discussed it with their parish priest who asked them to speak with the vocation director in the diocese.

The vocation director was pleased to receive Edward and his parents. He said that the best thing was for

Edward to finish his present education and then apply. He advised Edward to pray for the spirit to discern the will of God and his total willingness to go to the Seminary. He also advised him to be of good character and be serious with his studies. Edward was already intelligent. The moral values he learned from his parents already helped him to comport himself and dispose good character. His good academic report card in his present school was another factor. He could barely contain his excitement. He remembered that going to the Seminary will be the first time of going away from their family home. He thought about missing his parents and siblings. He knew that he would miss them a great deal but his passion to join the Seminary to serve overcomes his sadness for his family.

Edward later graduated from high school with excellent grades. Eddy and Cathy thought that he will forget about the Seminary, but they were wrong, his interest intensified. It was hard for Eddy and Cathy to allow Edward to leave their home and go to Seminary, they are aware that Edward's siblings will miss him dearly too. They later allowed him to follow his heart. They started making enquiries on how they can enrol him in a Seminary. They called the school and followed the due process of admission into the Seminary. Edward's good grades and character encouraged them to accept him in the Seminary. When they admitted him in the school, his joy knew no bounds. Before he left, he promised his parents to make them proud and to have good grades. Edward found the Seminary remarkably interesting. Though life in the Seminary was different from living his life at home with his siblings, he was ready to endure everything to achieve his goal.

The Seminary schedule was quite rigorous for Edward. They wake up early and start their activities each day. They are constantly busy doing one thing or the order. The little time he had for himself to rest was not enough and most times he used the resting period to read. His joy was that they pray in the Seminary. They have private time to pray and meditate. During meditation, he resumes his reflections and meditations on God's love for humanity. He often gazes and reflects on the cross. The more he reflects on how God gave himself up for torture and crucifixion for our redemption, the more he loves him and wants to suffer and die for him. He genuinely wanted to reciprocate God's love for humanity. He specifically loved adoration and meditation time. His resolve to suffer in return for God's love helped him endure the harshness of Seminary life. It gave him joy that he can be able to offer something for God. When he remembered that many saints died while proclaiming God's love, he was ready and eager to follow their footsteps.

Edward liked to read, and he likes reading the lives of the saints and the mystics of the Church. It gives him so much joy to read about these people who willingly suffered for God. They gave their lives serving God and defending their faith. These saints and saints in the making decided to die instead of committing sin, taking the easy way out or betraying God. Their sufferings and death remind Edward that he needs to offer his sufferings for the sins of the world just like his saint heroes did. Their sufferings remind him that many saints endured bigger pains and agony for Christ. He decided to endure and follow their footsteps. His life strategies and determination strengthened and encouraged him. It surprises other new Seminarians that Edward is indifferent to their complaints.

Within a few weeks, everyone knows Edward because of his constant questions in the class. He realized that the more he asks questions, the more he learns. He is ready to learn more about God so that he will serve him better. One of the Seminarians hated him for his questions in the class. He thought that Edward was trying to show off his intelligence. He disliked Edward's show of wisdom because he answered questions that most of them in the class were unable to answer. While Edward continued to excel in his studies and wisdom, he attracted several adversaries. Kevin was the worst among them. He disliked Edward and he was determined to frustrate him. Edward noticed that Kevin was always planning something mischievous against him. He tried to avoid him. Kevin set traps for Edward but in his wisdom, he escaped them, this infuriated Kevin so that he resorted to verbal attacks to Edward. It surprised Kevin that Edward never responded or tried to attack him back or report him.

The excessive bullying Edward received from Kevin intensified and sometimes he wanted to fight back but the picture of Jesus hanging on the cross kept coming to his mind. Secondly, he reminded himself that what he was going through in the hands of Kevin might be easier than what the saints and martyrs went through. He chose to tolerate Kevin. Edward's response to Kevin's futility angered him the more. He angrily bullied him more. Gradually, Edward began to become annoyed with Kevin. Though he tried to fight it, the feelings kept coming back. He decided to use the same method he used when he was young. He remembered that when he was young, and he refused to go to Church with his parents because the Church was boring to him. He decided to keep himself busy with things that are good in the Church, he discovered Jesus on the cross and kept meditating on him, he asked questions about why he must suffer on the cross with bleeding hands and legs. When his parents explained everything to him, he loved Jesus and that was part of the reasons why he came to the Seminary to reciprocate his love.

Edward studied Kevin and found out that he was not entirely a bad person. Kevin had notable talent of singing and playing music (piano and organ). Edward started admiring Kevin for all his talents. He decided to focus on the good side of Kevin and ignore his ugly side. He started praising God for his talents. As he focused more on his talents, he started liking him because he played music and praised God. Even though Kevin was becoming tired of disturbing Edward, whenever he pulls out his usual taunts, Edward remembered his musical talents, remembered the ridicule Jesus underwent and he calmed down. Edward later approached Kevin to teach him how to play musical instruments. Kevin was surprised at Edwards friendship despite his being mean to him. He reluctantly agreed to do that, and they later became friends. Though life was busy and tedious at the Seminary, Edward used his usual strategy to overcome challenges, in fact, he missed Seminary after they both graduated.

Chapter 5

Edward became a virtuous priest

Edward graduated from the Seminary, was first ordained a transitional Deacon, and later was ordained a diocesan priest. The joy of Eddy and Cathy knew no bounds. They were so happy and proud that their son became a priest. His siblings were overjoyed at his success as well. Fr. Edward visited and stayed with his family before celebrating his first Mass at his home parish. The day he celebrated his first Mass was remarkable for him. Their home Church brought back a flood of childhood memories. He remembered how he refused to enter the Church with his parents, and he laughed. During the procession into the Church, he looked at the cross and he almost melted down in tears. He remembered his childhood encounter with the big cross hanging in the Church. He remembered how he used to look at it to avoid boredom in the Church and eventually fall in love with it.

While processing to the altar, he looked around and remembered families in the pews. They were all happy to welcome him back to his home parish. The choir sang well as usual, and their presence reminded him of his childhood and his love for music. He used to listen to them in the Church to keep himself occupied. The Mass hymns that they sang were meaningful to him. He vowed in his mind to be a responsible, holy, and committed priest. The hymns further explained the sacredness of priesthood. In a flash, he looked at the organist, remembered Kevin, and smiled. Kevin should be in his home parish as well for his first Mass. Edward was able to preside over the Mass as if he had been saying Mass for years. He was prepared and everything went well. His parish priest in his home parish was well pleased.

The current parish priest in his home parish now was not the parish priest that was there when he went to the Seminary. He welcomed Fr. Edward and the congregation celebrated his priesthood. The parish presented him a gift and welcomed everyone to the parish hall for more celebration. The priest praised Eddy and Cathy for being good parents to Fr. Edward and for their continuous dedication and commitment to the Church. He praised them for allowing and supporting Edward to become a priest and encouraged everyone to pray for more priestly vocations. They later went to the parish hall and celebrated his priesthood at a parish banquet. Though Fr. Edward's first assignment as a parochial vicar in a parish was already known, the parishioners encouraged him to come back to his home parish as often as possible. Some people gave him gifts. They took some pictures with him before dismissal.

Edward spent a few days with his family before proceeding to his newly assigned parish. It was a memorable family reunion. Eddy and Cathy expressed their joy for Fr. Edwards priesthood. They told Fr. Edward that they are not surprised at his achievement. They have always known him to be a determined and hardworking person. They pleaded with him to keep up his virtuous deeds. Fr. Edward also thanked his parents for their love and support. His siblings were happy for him. They promised to visit him regularly in his new parish. Fr. Edward gave his family his priestly blessing before he left for his new parish and promised to communicate with them and to visit whenever possible.

They introduced Fr. Edward to the parishioners in his new parish, and they welcomed him. His first Mass went off without a hitch as if he had been celebrating Mass for years. During his homily the whole Church was so quiet that you could hear the pin drop. The amazing thing was that even children were calm. Many parishioners stood in line to welcome him and to congratulate him for his beautiful homily. He saw and greeted many parishioners that day. The next day was a weekday Mass. He was surprised to see many people in the Church. He admired their dedication and promised God to do his best and draw many souls to God.

The parish priest was very friendly and welcoming. He introduced Fr. Edward to the parish staff and the parish surroundings. He assigned him to supervise certain activities and works in the parish like the youth, burials etcetera. Edward did not hide his enthusiasm and maturity, and everyone loved him for that. He took his duties seriously. He does not take the preparation of his homily lightly. He closes his office door during the days he prepares his homily. The calmness of the surroundings enables him to meditate and prepare his homily. The parishioners look forward to his motivational homily. They often congratulate him after Mass for his homily. The day he said Mass with the parish priest, he marveled at his homily. The parish priest praised him for preparing such a touching homily.

Fr. Edward revealed that he always prays before his homilies. Most importantly, he prays before the Blessed Sacrament and asks for God's inspiration and guidance. He is also remarkably close to our Blessed Mother Mary. He calls on her to help him with her wisdom and intercession. God, through the intercession of our Blessed Mother Mary helps him with the preparation of his homily. He said that homilies are particularly important because they can inspire and save a lot of people. It is like a targeted message from God to the people of God. To prepare it well, you need God's intervention. It is interesting that Fr. Edward did not claim the glory, he attributed the glory to God and our Blessed Mother Mary.

His stay in his new parish was interesting and challenging to Fr. Edward. In as much as a lot of people love him, his knowledge and his homilies, there are a few parishioners who are looking for trouble. Some parishioners complain that Fr. Edward stays long during confessions before Mass. A man was incredibly angry because he came on time for confession before Mass, but he could not go because Fr. Edward saw only a few people that came before him. Fr. Edward does not want to rush people during confession. He likes to talk to them and counsel to help them. When the man eventually confronted him with arrogance, he calmly explained to the man that confession is a sacrament which should not be rushed, he explained the reasons why he does not rush confessions. The man apologized to him for his tone of voice.

Fr. Edward applied all the virtues he acquired from childhood, from his parents, in the Seminary to tackle any issues that arises. There was a time the parish priest went away and entrusted the parish in his hands. He was able to discharge his duties responsibly. Those who look for trouble, he ignores and looks beyond the person to admire the handiwork of God.

If that did not work, he remembers the cross and what Jesus Christ went through. The parishioners loved him because of his calm demeanor and the way he manages contentious issues. He stayed only one year in that parish, and the chancery office posted him as a parish priest to a parish that needed a priest urgently. They believed he could manage a parish because of his maturity and based on recommendations written by his first parish priest.

Through Fr. Edward's homilies and strategies, people returned to the Church and new people started attending Mass in their Church. The parishioners were amazed at the sharp increase in Church attendance. As people talk to their friends in other parishes people come to their Church and when they come, they liked the homilies, and they decided to continue to attend Masses in their Church. The bishop was impressed with his progress and the increase in the money they submit to the Diocese. The progress of the Church even reflects in the money they submit to the Diocese.

Fr. Edward stayed long in that parish and the parishioners especially the youth love him and want him to stay forever. He used all the skills he learned from his new experience concerning the youth in his former parish as the parish vicar. He explained that the youth are the heart of the Church, and they should be encouraged and supported. He often told stories of his childhood experience in the Church. The stories touched many people, and they learned from them. They learned to appreciate everyone, they learned to praise the good things in people, to forgive people and look up to the cross as our point of reference in our difficulties and sorrows of life.

Many parishioners asked him to be their spiritual director. They learned a lot from his homilies and wanted him to extend the guidance in their spirituality. Edward tried as much as he can to attend to their spiritual needs. He also built up a strong volunteer group that takes care of the poor and hungry in the Church. He not only takes care of their spiritual need; he also takes care of their poverty and hunger problems. The parishioners marvel at the level of growth in their Church since the arrival of Fr. Edward. He also built a gigantic statue of our Blessed Mother Mary and encouraged devotions to our Blessed Mary in their Parish. The parishioners talk about his miraculous gifts. The more they talk about it, the more people flock into their parish.

The most important thing they love about him is that he loves, appreciates everyone, he raises people's self-confidence. People rarely talk about suicide in their Church community because he makes them love themselves and appreciate life itself. They love his faith that there is something good and admirable about each person and when you discover something good, you praise the good things, you should remember the good things, and forget about the negative aspect of the person because with time the bad characteristics of the person will vanish. The person that people praise and appreciate is motivated to do better things.

Chapter 6

Edward's popular homily that converted people

Fr. Edward's popular homilies that he repeatedly preaches are based on childhood experiences that helped him. He explained that part of the reason he made the decision was because many people had shared with him the benefits of such homilies. Many people had told him how such homilies changed their lives for good. He analyzed his experience and brought out the major lessons he learned from his experience as a child. He analyzed how those lessons and virtues helped him. For instance, he found the Mass too boring that he decided not to go to Church again. He argued with his parents, but they explained to him that going to Mass was non-negotiable. When he realized that they meant every word he decided to appreciate the good things he found in the Church so that he would not be bored.

He realized that the more he appreciated and admired those things he started falling in love with them. He has applied this way of experiencing life situations and it has helped him. The lesson is to find something interesting and fascination about people, places, or things. Fr. Edward learned that God wants us to love everyone just like He loves us and when we do not like someone, we should try our best to find something interesting about that person, appreciate the person for their talent, praise the person and that eventually we start loving the person as an important creature of God.

Fr. Edward preached that there is something good about everyone. He explained that it is better to be positive than to be negative. He taught that God endowed everyone with talents and when we appreciate such talent in the person, the person will tend to bring out or develop even more talent. He also talked about the importance of humility, he stated that when we are humble, we will be able to learn good things from other people. He stated that it is not good to give up easily on people because God did not give up on us. Giving up on people is like abandoning God's creature without trying to explore the good things about them. He explained that it is not good to dwell on the boring or negative aspect of someone's character but to focus on the good things instead.

He said that he is thankful that his parents taught him how to pray. He appreciated the fact that his parents did not allow him to have his way. He realized that if his parents gave up and allowed him stay at home, he would not have been who he is today. He encouraged parents to set standing principles and high standards for their children in their homes. He encouraged parents to make rules and regulations that will benefit their children and families, starting with daily prayer and Mass should be at the top list. He reminds them of the popular saying that the family that prays together, stays together. He further explains that the graces they receive from such prayers will transform their lives for the better. He reminded parents about their responsibility to raise their children in the fear of God. He said that it might be hard, but they need to start when their children are still young and be consistent. They should also model good behaviors to the children who learn by watching.

Fr. Edward explained that he fell in love with the image of Jesus hanging on the cross in his childhood. He explained that as his parents being devout Catholics, insisted that he should stay calm during Mass. And while looking around the Church to find something that can capture his eyes and imagination, he saw Jesus hanging on the cross and pitied him. In his curiosity, he inquired what crime he committed. When his parents explained what Jesus did for us, he started loving him. He started focusing on Jesus and, he started consoling him in his mind. The more he gazed at him, the more he loved him and wanted to come to Mass to gaze at him. He explained that when he grew up, he still gazed at Jesus, and he mostly went to him for deeper healing conversation. He encouraged everyone to love Jesus, to appreciate him, to look up to him during difficult situations of life.

He taught that from his experience, he learned that if you genuinely want to come close to Jesus, you will go through his cross. The more he looks at Jesus on the cross, he meditates on his pains, the more he knows and feels his pain, the more he loves him, the more he yearns to make him happy and making him happy to relieve his pain, means to stay away from sin. Staying away from sin connects and bonds him with God in a way that the happiness he feels is indescribable and he does not fear death anymore because death will only take him to the one, he loves. He encouraged people to follow in the same footsteps. He confidently says that they will not regret it. He further urges people to go to Jesus on the cross and Jesus in the Blessed Sacrament as their refuge and strength.

He ends by reminding them to love everyone, to see something good in people, to appreciate something good, to praise something good and ignore the negative aspect of people. He says that if they do not appreciate, admire, or love people, neighbors, friends, brothers, and sisters that they see or things that God made, how can they claim to love God that they do not see. He teaches that love supersedes everything. He explains that he is talking from experience because when he realized as a child that admiring other things in the Church helped him to discover a lot of beautiful things going on in the Church including the music, altar servers which he later joined to serve his newfound friend Jesus hanging on the cross. He later applied the same lesson in all the places where he worked. He learned never to hate rather; he discovered a lot of talents that helped him in his previous parishes. He learned to have a forgiving spirit like Jesus hanging on the cross. He forgives people when they offend him especially when he remembers that Jesus equally forgave all the atrocities committed against him.

Chapter 7

Edward's experiences saved Mark and Magi from divorce

Magi, you started again, why did you keep these dirty plates in the living room? Why are you lazy? Mark concluded. Screaming from the kitchen, Magi said, you called me lazy, you dirty man. Mark became angrier, he rushed to the kitchen to confront Magi. Magi saw him coming and grabbed a kitchen knife and warned Mark that if he dares touches her, she will stab him. Mark looked at her and shouted, I hate you so much. Magi filled with so much anger and hatred screamed back, I hate you too. Mark looked at her for a moment and quietly said. I wonder what I am still doing with you, I will file for divorce. Magi did not hesitate, she replied, sounds good and be fast about it.

I will do that as soon as possible, said Mark, heading to his room, he continued to scream in anger. His phone started ringing and when he picked up, he screamed with joy. An old friend called him to invite him and Magi to their son's wedding. He looked at his calendar and assured the friend that he will be able to attend the wedding. He told the friend that he would like him to call Magi himself and inform her. Their mutual friend later called Magi and Magi accepted the invitation to attend the wedding. On the wedding day, Mark and Magi attended the wedding but they did not come together, they came in their separate cars. Mark arrived first, exchanged pleasantries, and sat down. When Magi entered the Church, she saw Mark and wanted to sit in another place, suddenly she thought about what her friends will say. She dragged herself and sat beside Mark without uttering a word to him. Magi sat with Mark because one of her friends had sarcastically made disparaging comments about her marriage to Mark. Magi looked at her friend and smiled as if everything was okay. Mark was surprised to see Magi by his side but ignored her.

Fortunately, it was Fr. Edward that presided the wedding. Mark and Magi are Catholics, but they are not serious with their faith. They only go to Church occasionally. However, they still recognized Fr. Edward as a devout, and nice priest. Shortly after their arrival, the Mass started, and Fr. Edward thanked all of them for coming. He congratulated the couple for deciding to get married in the Church. During homily, Fr. Edward explained that marriage is a Sacrament, and we should respect it. He indicated that since marriage is not a child's play, couples that are planning to get married need to be in love with each other. He explained that marriage is like the marriage of Christ to the Church. Christ loves the Church, and he gave his life for the Church. The same way husbands and wives are supposed to love each other, offer sacrifices and be ready to die for each other regardless of the situation, whether in sickness or good health.

As Fr. Edward continued, he emphasized that husbands should love their wives and not be harsh with them. When he said that, Magi stole a look at her husband and silently signed sarcastically. Mark looked at her and waved his head in pity and mumbled "this woman will not change; she is fighting even in the Church." Fr. Edward also said that wives are supposed to be obedient to their husbands. Immediately Mark silently giggled without looking at Magi. Magi ignored him and kept looking at Fr. Edward with interest. Her gaze at Fr. Edward seem to show that she was not aware of whatever was happening around her. When Mark noticed that Magi did not respond to him. He looked at her intently and noticed that she was extremely interested in what Fr. Edward was saying. He started looking intently to find out what is catching Magi's interest. As he started listening more attentively, Fr. Edward started talking about his childhood experiences that couples could apply to sustain their marriage.

Fr. Edward explained that if married couples want their marriage to last, they should start with God, pray to God together and the graces obtained from prayers will sustain their love for each other. They should bear in mind that their love is like delicate flower which supposed to nurture, water, and carefully taken care of. He continued that when the love is waning, you should remember all those things that made you fall in love with the person. Remember the good memories and old days. Remember those racing hearts of love. If those things are no longer there, take time to look anew at your wife or your husband, and rediscover the many good things you each have to offer. Admire again those talents, appreciate them, and declare your love for such talents and thank God the creator. Fr. Edward said many more things and then concluded by telling the would be married couples and all the married couples in the Church to close their eyes for few minutes, think and remember only the pleasant things about their spouse and places they have been together, the good memories they have shared. Fr. Edward stopped talking and started praying silently for them.

When he continued the Mass, Magi was already crying silently. She remembered many good things about Mark. She remembered the first time they met and how loving, and caring Mark was and how he showered her with so much love and gifts. She tried to remember how their problems started. As she was thinking, uncontrollable tears kept rolling down her face. Mark also remembered many good things about Magi. He also remembered how they started and how he loved Magi so much and he could not pinpoint the reason he hated her so much now. "It may be because of her bad choice of language? No, the priest told us to remember only the good things." When he remembered the good, tasty meals Magi prepares without receiving much appreciation from him, he felt bad. He looked at Magi and saw the tears rolling down her face, he felt so sorry for the good things she does without receiving appreciation from him, he hugged her and wiped her face. Magi cried the more, leaned on him and told him that she is sorry for being inconsiderate. It was as if God removed the selfish pride in them and replaced it with love. Mark held her, looked at her and said, "I love you honey" and Magi quickly replied leaning on him again "I love you." They were so happy. It was not only Mark and Magi, that the meditation helped, it really evoked a lot of memories and emotions among many couples in the Church. Fr. Edward was amazed at their reaction.

At the end of the Mass, Mark and Magi went and thanked Fr. Edward for saving their marriage. They briefly told him that they nearly filed for divorce. They also thanked their friend for inviting them to the wedding. Many couples came and thanked Fr. Edward for his homily. They expressed how recharged they are and that they are ready to improve and sustain their marriage. They told Fr. Richard that they have learned a lot of things that will enhance their marriage. Mark and Magi went home and started a second honeymoon. They made a resolution to start taking their prayers seriously and they did. They started saying Rosary together before bedtime. They always attend Sunday Mass and attend weekday Masses when it is possible for them. They learned a lot from Fr. Edwards homily, they applied it and it is working for them. Life always brings challenges, but they have been happily married without many issues because they have developed coping mechanisms. It was as if Fr. Edward opened their eyes to things, they took for granted. They started expressing their love for each other and to appreciate each other.

Chapter 8

Edward's experience helped Charity, a young girl

Lindsay was born into a rich family. She was an only child and her parents pampered her so much that she got whatever she wanted. When she was in seventh grade in a good school, saw other children, whose parents were not as rich as her parents, she felt superior to them. Ebony and her mom just moved to the area near Lindsay's school and her mom had to enrol Ebony in that school. The day Ebony entered Lindsay's classroom, Lindsay looked at everything she was wearing and realized that she came from a poor family. She chose to distance herself from Ebony even though she sat beside her. Whenever Ebony greeted or asked her any questions, she ignored her and pretended not to understand what she was talking about. Ebony felt extremely uncomfortable by her side. Her problem heightened when she wanted to play with Lindsay's group of friends, Lindsay rudely humiliated her and warned her to stay off. Ebony wanted to report Lindsay and her friends to the school authorities. However, she changed her mind knowing that Lindsay might make life even more unbearable for her in the school. The incident made her so moody even when her mom picked her up after school, she was still gloomy.

Ebony told her mom that she would like to stop going to that school. Her mom wanted to know the reason she said that, but she was not ready to talk about what happened. When she finished eating, her mom explained to her that she would have liked to grant her request but unfortunately that school was the only good school close to where they live and her place of work.

Ebony later opened up and described all that happened to her mom. She wanted a change of class because she can no longer tolerate Lindsay's humiliation and intimidation. When she insisted, her mom came to the school and pleaded with the school authority to send her daughter to another class. When she mentioned Lindsay's name, the principal of the school was not surprised because they have had similar cases in the past. He changed Ebony to another calmer class where she felt much better. At least students in that class treated her like human being.

The school contacted Lindsay's parents and reported the incident to them. They felt so bad about it. They were not in support of Lindsay's conduct. They grounded Lindsay for her actions and warned her that if she continues, they will remove a lot of privileges. Lindsay hated Ebony for reporting her to her parents and she planned to retaliate. She got the chance the day all the seventh graders went out on excursion. Lindsay used any opportunity to silently insult and call Ebony names. She told Ebony that it was because of her that her parents punished her. As usual Ebony did not respond to her. She ignored her and remained focused on why they came. Ebony's inability to respond to her further infuriated Lindsay. She wanted to verbally attack her but realized that Ebony had gotten a lot of friends from her new class. They were ready to defend her.

Lindsay's family go to Church mostly on occasions like Christmas, Easter, and other important solemnities in the Church. During Easter of that year. When Lindsay's Dad travelled, her mom went to the Church with her. Fr. Edward was the presider. His usual homily based on his life experience did the wonders again. The part that touched Lindsay was when Fr. Edward mentioned that there is something good in everyone and if one hates something, try, and look around the person and you must surely find something interesting about the person. She remembered Ebony and what she has done. However, she remembered that Ebony was proficient in Mathematics and sports, 3897798and she was not. She thought about it for a while and concluded that Fr. Edward was right. She also remembered that Fr. Edward explained that we all are the creatures of God, that no one is more important than the other person. He further explained that we should be compassionate to those we meet, that we should show love to everyone despite his or her background.

Lindsay felt so bad. She asked her mom to help her arrange to go for confession. Her mom was surprised because she had been persuading her to go to confession for a long time and she had been sarcastically saying that she has not sinned. The last time she went to confession was when she received her first Holy Communion. Her mom was genuinely happy when she mentioned confession. She promised her that after the Mass she will wait for her to go to confession. Her mom kept on thinking about what may have propelled her into wanting to go to confession so bad. She remembered that Fr. Edward emphasized the importance of going to confession especially the Easter season. After Mass, they went to the confessional and wait in line to go to confession. After the confession Lindsay felt much better. She told her mom that Fr. Edward's homily truly touched her. She promised her mom that she will apologize to Ebony for being rude to her.

Lindsay waited so eagerly for morning so that she can go to school and apologize to Ebony. Unfortunately for her Ebony did not come to school that day. Ebony came to school the next day and she hugged her. Ebony did not expect such behavior from Lindsay, and she wondered if she was all right.

Lindsay took Ebony out in a corner and apologized to her. She told her that she was sorry for the way she treated her. Ebony started crying and Lindsay asked her for a long time the reason she was crying, and Ebony explained that her father passed, and he had been a rich man. She remembered how he pampered and loved her. After the incident, Lindsay and Ebony became friends in school and at home. Their friendship connected the two families. Ebony was able to help Lindsay in many ways. She taught Lindsay how to study and learn math and sciences. She also exposed Lindsay to sports. When they graduated from school, Ebony became a star in numerous sports which fetched her a lot of money. Since she was earning a lot of money, she encouraged her mom to stop working so she can rest. Lindsay in her corner was doing good too. She credited Fr. Edward for helping her become a better person.

Chapter 9

Edwards Experience helped teacher and Joe

David had been a teacher for 20 years. Teaching was a cultural capital in his family. David's father was a teacher. David was a professional teacher but since a particular boy joined their school, he faced a huge challenge in his life. He sometimes preferred to call in sick to avoid the boy's trouble. He struggled so hard to hold himself so that the boy will not aggravate him. The boy's name was Joe. Joe had indeed proven to be a terror in the school. He moved from one school to another. Sometimes he was not intentionally naughty, he just could not hold or control himself. Since David started teaching, he had been encountering various kinds of overactive students, but Joe was so challenging even for him. For the first time in his teaching history, the principal warned David to stop raising his voice at students. For the first time in his teaching career, he wanted to stay at home for some time to think and avoid Joe's problems. He took that decision because Joe nearly pushed him to use unprofessional word, hit or scream at him. Initially, David used a low tone of voice on Joe, but Joe gets even worse. He was always ready to verbally fight anyone that gets close to him.

A single mom raised Joe. His dad left his mom when he was born. He grew up with much hatred for his dad. Being a single mom raising her child alone, Joe's mom did not have sufficient time to spend quality time with Joe. She worked two jobs to able to take care of Joe and their bills. Joe felt abandoned by his dad and his mom did not show him the love and time he craved for. Even though his mom tried her best to provide and care for Joe, he was not satisfied with his mom's efforts.

Joe often goes to school with bitterness streaming from his ugly arguments with his mom. When he gets to school, he transfers it to the teachers especially to David. Joe has another active friend in the class. They disobey the teachers and distract other students in the classroom. The worst case was when other students realizing that Joe gets away with his naughty behavior joined Joe and the classroom became as noisy as marketplace. Before Joe joined the school, the students were normally well behaved. They followed instructions to the core but when David lost control of the class to avoid attracting the principal who had warned him to be careful with what he says to the students, the students play in class without much control.

David obtained the permission to take off a few days. David used to go to Church but with his teaching schedule, he stopped going. His days off gave him opportunities to go to Church. David hated Joe so much. He cannot even control the anger in his heart. He just wanted to feel better; he wanted to go and pray to God for forgiveness. When he arrived at the Church, he met very few people praying in the pews while waiting for the priest to start the Mass. David looked at the flowers before the Altar and they were so beautiful. While pondering on the beauty of the flower and the generosity of those that kept and beautified the church, the choir began to sing. Everyone stood up and became to sing. David stood up and looked at the back and saw Fr. Edward in the procession, he smiled. He loved Fr. Edward and his famous homilies. He admitted that he really needed such homilies to put his sanity intact. After the Mass, David went home inspired by what he heard from Fr. Edward in the Church. He had heard before that showing love was particularly important, but the way Fr. Edward explained it was quite different and practical.

David went back to school a different person. He realized that he has not been patient with Joe. He also admitted that the behavior of Joe infuriated him, he hated him, and he raised his voice at him. He thought that raising his voice at Joe will make him keep quite like the other students. The first day David returned to school, he looked at Joe with different eye. Eye of compassion and love. Remembering all that Fr. Edward said, he called Joe and asked him how he was fairing. David told him that he missed him. Joe wanted to be angry because he thought David was being sarcastic, but when he looked at David's face, he realized that he was not joking. It melted his heart, Joe came close to David and said that he was sorry for all he had done. David looked at Joe and told him that he should not worry because he still loves him. Hearing that word "love" Joe turned at David, gazed at him intently, wanted to say something but he smiled at him and left. David noticed that Joe was calm in the class. He seemed to be thinking about something deep. David realized that Fr. Edward was right when he said that love begets love and hate produces hatred.

David realized that when Joe was calm, the whole class was calm. He then focused on Joe, trying to reassure him that he is important and special to him. He over praised him for doing anything good. The more David praised Joe, the more he becomes better emotionally, physically, and academically. Joe went home and bragged about David, how he was his best friend and teacher. Joe's mom came to the school and thanked David for bringing his boy back to reality. One day, David had a doctor's appointment and could not come to school. Joe missed him so much that he kept asking when David will come back. He really wanted to tell David something important. David came to school the next day, Joe ran and hugged him. He asked him "do you really mean it when you say that you love me?" David told him that he meant every word, Joe asked him "do you think my dad loves me?" Your dad, how do you mean? David asked. My dad, my dad, Joe stuttered. David said, "look at me dear, I am your friend, you can trust me, tell me about your dad." My dad abandoned us "mom said that he cannot come back and see me, and I am so sad, I really want to have a dad" Joe said, almost crying.

David looked at Joe with so much love and pity. He wanted to cry with him but controlled himself. He kept comforting Joe and he assured him that things will be all right. He now understood the reasons behind Joe's character. He realized why Joe had been so bitter. David intensified his love for Joe. He listened to him anytime he needed his attention.

One beautiful cool morning, Joe came to David and asked him, "can you be my dad? Please do not say no." David was shocked, he was short of words, he could not express his shock. He looked at Joe and explained that it does not work that way. David clarified to Joe that it will be a discussion between him and his mother. My mom? Shouted Joe. Wait, I can call her and tell her that you want to be my dad, she will agree, trust me. Before David can utter a word, Joe ran to the office to ask the receptionist that he needed to tell her mom something important. David still dumbfounded could not say anything. He did not know whether to be angry or happy. He had lost his wife a long time ago and he was not planning to marry any time soon. As he was still thinking, Joe hurriedly rushed back to the class and told David that his mom was at work and will speak with him in the evening. David opened his mouth to say something but could not say anything. He was just gazing at Joe. Not knowing what to do, he dismissed him with a wave of hand. After few minutes, Joe knocked at his head and came to David. I forgot to collect your telephone number. "What for, Joe? David asked. "I need your telephone number so that I can call you in the evening, mom will call you, remember?" David told him that he will speak with him later.

David went home and spent the whole evening thinking about what Joe told him. He did not want to get married after the death of his wife. On the other hand, he did not want to spoil the happy turnaround in Joe's life. He did not give Joe his number and he was not expecting his call. Even though he was not expecting Joe's call, his heart went out to him in pity and wished he could call him. Joe went home so chartered and sick. David knew the kind of sickness Joe was going through and he felt sorry for him. His mom called school the next day to say that Joe will not be able to come to school because he was sick. Joe told his mom that he was deceived by David who promised to love him.

He described to his mom, how he had asked David to be his dad. His mom screamed "are you serious, how can you ask him to be your dad?" Joe softly screamed back, "I need dad, mom, he loves me, and I love him but he, he, he refused to give me his number" After a few minutes Joe said, "do you think he will accept to be my dad?" Joe's mom had seen how desperate Joe was and told him that he can ask David when he sees him. Joe jumped and said that he was feeling better, and he wanted to go to school. When he kept on disturbing his mom, she took him to school. On entering the school, Joe's mom met David walking on the hallway. Joe saw him and ran after him. He stopped David and hugged him. He introduced his mom to David, and they exchanged greetings while looking at each other in the eyes.

David could not concentrate after meeting with Joe's mom. Her eyes kept flashing in his mind. On the other hand, Joe's mom was blushing at work and her friend colleague asked her if she found a new friend. She was surprised that her friend noticed something. She tried to distract herself but could not. David did not hesitate to give Joe his number when he asked again. Later that evening, Joe did not ask permission from his mom before calling David. David secretly had been longing for Joe's call. He still could not explain what was wrong with him.

As he was still thinking about the whole episode, his phone began to ring, he grabbed it and without even looking, he said, "hi Joe, how is your mom?" a familiar voice from the phone startled David "who is Joe?" asked David's mom who has been bugging David to get married and give her grandchildren. David gently told his mom that he will call her later because he was expecting a call. As her mom was still talking, Joe's call started coming, David picked up and greeted Joe. He asked Joe to pass the phone to his mom. Joe's mom eagerly received the phone and was beaming with smiles. David asked her if they can eat out that weekend. She agreed and Joe was incredibly happy.

David formerly adopted Joe as his child, and he was super excited to have David as his dad. Joe turned to be completely a lovely kid. It showed that he had been going though emotional trauma because of the absence of a dad in his life. Considering the love at first sight that existed between David and Joe's mom, they got married few months after. Since Joe's mom was not formerly married to Joe's biological dad, it was easy for them to get married in the Church. Their wedding day in the Church was so remarkable because the dramatic change in David and Joe began with Fr. Edward's popular homily from his childhood experiences in the Church. David made out time to explain and thank Fr. Edward for helping him unite with this wonderful family. The important thing about Fr. Edward was that he was humble to the core, he always gave the glory to God. He said "I always pray before my homilies and beg God to use me as an instrument to touch the hearts of people so that their hearts will understand and accept the lessons from the day's liturgy. Joe and his mom moved to David's big beautiful white house which was closer to their school. One year later, Joe's mom gave birth to a set of twins, a boy, and a girl. David's mom was happy for having many grand children in such a short while.

Chapter 10

Edward's experience encouraged family prayer

Tony and his wife Ruth got married and soon God blessed them with one child. They wanted to have more children but could not. Tony and Ruth really wanted a large family since Tony was the only child of his parents. He wanted many children around him. Whenever Ruth sees other families with children, she admired them and wanted to be like them. Rose, their only child had grown and had been disturbing them to get a child for her. Ruth kept on having miscarriages. When she was pregnant, she celebrated with her husband but after few months, Ruth dreamed of a monster who chased her in the dream and in the morning, she had a miscarriage. This experience had happened for three consecutive years.

Rose on the other hand had been having nightmares. She screamed in the middle of the night and ran to the room Tony and Ruth shared together. She described a monster that chased her in her dream. The description matches the same experience as Ruth. The only difference was that Ruth usually had such nightmares when she was pregnant. When Rose's constant nightmares continued, Tony and Ruth became worried because they are losing their daughter gradually. Rose does not sleep well, and it affects her daily activities including school activities. Her situation worsened when she cannot stay alone in a place. She follows her parents everywhere for fear of seeing the monster again. In the classroom, she withdrew herself, and one can easily detect that something was wrong with her.

Tony and Ruth used to be committed to Church activities but could not keep up because of their tight work schedule. The activities happening in their house worried them and they thought the best place to turn was to turn to God. And the best way to tell God was to go to Mass. They were happy to hear Fr. Edwards homily the Sunday they attended Mass. They were able to learn how to take family prayers seriously. They regretted not starting the family prayer tradition right on their wedding night. After the Mass, Tony and Ruth took Rose to Fr. Edward. They asked him to pray for Rose and Ruth for their nightmares. They explained everything they have been going through. Fr. Edward

Prayed for them and asked them when they started experiencing the nightmares. Tony and Ruth thought about it and answered that it was when they got their new house after their wedding. Fr. Edward said that he will come and bless the house. He encouraged them to go to Mass, have family prayers together and should be saying the Rosary and the prayer to St. Michael. He gave them Holy Water they can sprinkle everywhere in their house. He also reminded them not to be afraid and they should place their trust and hope in God. Fr. Edward later came and blessed their house as he promised.

Surprisingly, Rose's nightmares ceased. She did not see the monsters anymore. Gradually, her fears of staying alone vanished. Tony, Ruth, and Rose intensified their prayers. The more they intensified their prayers, the more they make out time for God and go to Church. They are mostly happy because they were free from the problems Rose had been going through. They were happy that God rescued them. Rose went to school and behaved better than she used to. Her teachers and students were surprised at her sudden change in attitude. She was no longer moody and miserable. They also noticed that she prays a lot. She prays before she eats, she also prays at the beginning of their class and at the end. Tony and Ruth were very impressed with their daughters love for prayers. There was a day they were super hungry and wanted to eat, Rose softly reminded Tony that they have not prayed when Tony had taken one spoon of food in his mouth. He apologized and patiently waited and ate after the prayers.

One hot breezy afternoon, Ruth came back from work so tired and uncomfortable. She managed to eat something before heading to their room to have short snap. As she was getting to the room, she started throwing up. When Tony came in and saw her throwing up, he told her to dress up so that they can go to the hospital. Tony took Ruth to the hospital, and they found out that Ruth was pregnant. They were happy about the news but when they remembered their previous ugly experiences, they shuddered. However, when they remembered the words of Fr. Edward who advised them not to be afraid. They did not relent in their prayers; they increased their prayers and Masses. Even if they were tired, their daughter will always remind them. Rose was joyful when she heard that she will soon have a sibling. She kept on dancing, touching, and pointing at Ruth's stomach. "I love you my little sister," said Rose. "Sister? how are you sure she is a girl? said Ruth smiling.

Months later, Ruth delivered twins, a boy, and a girl. They were exceedingly happy to welcome their babies. The interesting thing that happened was that Tony and Ruth introduced the twins to the importance of prayer right in the womb. They seemed to have learned from the womb because they love to pray. They also learned a lot of prayers from Rose their sister. As they were still enjoying the twins, Ruth got pregnant again and delivered a baby boy. In the end, Tony and Ruth have five children. God answered their prayers of having big family. Tony and Ruth were grateful to God for answering their prayers. They dedicated their life and family to God. Promising God to always make out time to worship him and to keep a lasting family prayer tradition. They were thankful to Fr. Edward whom God used to help a lot of families and individuals.

Chapter 11

Edward's experience helped Mike

Mike had not been lucky with relationships. Mike had two women that he wanted to Marry but they broke up in the end. He absolutely loved them, but it did not quite work for them, He gave up and declared to his friends that he will not fall in love again and he will take his career more seriously. Financially, Mike was doing well, but he was not happy. Megan joined their company and Mike was working closely with her. After a few months they fell in love with each other. However, Mike was sceptical about love because of his previous experiences. Megan really loved Mike and wanted to marry him. Mike did not want the relationship to be intimate for fear of heartbreak. As time went on Megan proved to Mike that she loved him. Mike decided to give love a chance. He officially proposed to marry Megan and the wedding preparation began.

Mike was so happy that at last he has fallen in love again. His family and friends were happy for him. One week before the wedding, Mike came back from work and was planning to call Megan to finalize their wedding plans, his phone started ringing. He picked up the phone and got the shock of his life. He received information that Megan had a terrible accident, and the hospital needed his attention. Mike abandoned everything and ran to the hospital. On reaching the hospital, he asked the doctor what happened. He wanted to see Megan, but they could not allow him to see her. They took Megan to the ICU for serious medical attention. They told him that he could see Megan shortly. Mike was pacing up and down the hospital's hallway when the Nurse called his attention. He went in and nearly fainted at what he saw. Megan sustained serious injuries during the accident. She saw Mike and tears rolled down her eyes. She gestured on Mike to come closer to her. Mike was still in shock, but he managed to drag himself to Megan, tears uncontrollably rolled down his eyes.

They kept on crying and holding each other for a long time. Megan stopped crying and was staying still. Mike rushed to get the Nurse; he pressed the bell. The Nurse examined her and told Mike that Megan has gone back to coma. The Nurse explained to Mike that Megan had been unconscious, but she just came out of it before he walked in. Mike came close to her and pleaded with her to come back to him. As he was crying and pleading with Megan, he felt her hand on his head. He looked at her at once. Megan smiled, looked at him and with shaking lips, said, "I love you so much Mike."

Mike was happy that she was out of coma and as he wanted to tell Megan that he loves her so much, she closed her eyes. While he was still battling with the situation, the Nurse told him that she is sorry about what happened. What happened? Inquired Mike. The Nurse explained to Mike that Megan is gone. Mike instantly fainted that they had to admit him to the hospital. He felt so bad and wanted to die. He remembered the hardships and heartbreaks through which he had passed. Now that he met a nice lady that loves him and was ready to marry him, she died. When he recovered from the shock, he cried like a baby. He blamed himself for breaking his promise. He blamed himself for fallen in love again. He convinced himself that something was wrong with him.

He refused to listen to anybody that tried to console him. It took him months to recover from the shock of Megan's death. One of his friends advised him to meet with a therapist to help him come back to reality. As they were discussing about which therapist to see. Knowing Fr. Edward, one of his friends told them that it will be better for Mike to see Fr. Edward. Mike belonged to another parish, and he did not know Fr. Edward. They scheduled appointment for Mike to meet with him. Mike's appointment was in the morning, so he decided to attend Mass. Surprisingly, he felt much better before meeting Fr. Edward in his office. His homily already did the magic. Mike explained everything that had happened in his life.

He even described what happened in his life when he was younger. When he was younger, he dreamt about serving God as a priest. He grew up and forgot about it because he did not take the dream seriously. Fr, Edward told him that he will need to come close to God to find out what God wanted from him. He told Mike that based on his story, God might be calling him to work for him in a unique way. However, he cannot conclude anything for now. He advised him to give more time to God, praying, going to Mass, and serving God.

Mike continued praying and the more he prays, the more he loves God, the more he wants to serve him. He felt so good with his newfound interest. He had never felt the way he was feeling. Even with Megan, he did not feel this way. He convinced himself that God might be calling him to be a priest. He went and told Fr. Edward about his decision to become a priest. Fr. Edward prayed for him and explained the process to him. Mike made inquiries, studied, and later joined the diocesan priests. He reflected and realized that God works in mysterious ways. He calls us in diverse ways. God can also use any situation to bring us closer him.

Mike admitted that if he had succeeded in the previous relationships or marriage with Megan, he would have missed his real vocation to serve God as a priest. He reflected that many people in the world might be going through the same problem of wrong choices. Mike remembered the story of his friend Dave who did not pray for God's guidance before getting married to his first wife. He remembered how Dave would have had heart attack from all the fights with her. Dave started having high blood pressure and he nearly died. The wife thinking that he will die, divorced him, and moved out of their house. Dave prayed and waited for so long before God blessed him with his current wife. After the annulment process, they got married in the church. They love each other so much and most importantly; they pray and go close to God.

Mike linked the experience of his friend to his own experience and concluded that being close to God and asking God to help us in whatever we are doing is the best approach in life. He explained that Dave would have died because of wrong choice. He is happy with his new wife; he is ready to take and endure anything that comes out of it knowing that it was God's choice for him. On the other hand, Mike was happy with his decision to serve God as a priest, and he is ready to take and endure anything that comes with it knowing fully well that God called him to serve him. He remembered the submission of Jesus to His father's will. Jesus suffered so much on the cross but knowing that it was the will of God the Father for him, he willingly accepted it, came to earth, taught about the kingdom of God, did everything that he was required to do, when the time came for him to sacrifice himself, he endured all the sufferings, died and entered his glory.

Mike was grateful how Fr. Edward was able to help him in his situation. He appreciated how Fr. Edwards's homilies and life story helped him, but the most important aspect of the healing therapy was gazing and focusing on the cross of Jesus. While looking at Jesus on the cross, he fell in love with him for suffering so much for our salvation. He learned a lot from Jesus. He realized that Jesus did not complain nor gave up despite the terrible situation he found himself. Mike explained that the words of Divine Mercy Prayer truly encouraged him. He said that the part that did the magic was the prayer that he said that we should not despair nor become despondent, but we should with great confidence trust and submit ourselves to the will and mercy of God.

Mike showed that the prayer and meditation on the sufferings of Jesus on the cross helped him when he was mourning the death of Megan. He started viewing death in another way, he realized that all would die someday but the most important thing was that we should focus on how to do the will of God, love and serve God so that we will be with God when we die. He promised to pray for Megan that God will forgive and receive her spirit and as for him, he has decided to give his heart and life to God and this decision gives him joy.

Just like Fr. Edward who used his childhood experiences to teach, preach and help many people, Mike decided to use his life experiences to instruct other people about the will of God. He decided to teach people that the will of God is the best and we should always pray and ask for God's will and merciful love in our lives. He concluded that if we resolutely pursue our own will without considering the will of God, we will never find true peace and happiness. Mike remembered how he eagerly wanted to marry and have children but now he will have more children as a priest because he will have time to help many children. He was determined to follow in the footsteps of Fr. Edward, since he was always joyful for being able to help many people. Mike wished that other people would do the same. He wished that we all will reflect, learn, and help others from our childhood or our past experiences.

Chapter 12

Another milestone in Edward's life

One sunny breezy beautiful afternoon, a senior priest from the same diocese came for a visit. Fr. Edward was happy to see the priest, but he was surprised to see the priest. However, he welcomed and entertained the priest. The priest did not immediately disclose to Fr. Edward the reasons for his visit, he relaxed and waited before giving the letter to Edward. He explained that the letter came from the bishop. He encouraged Fr. Edward to open the letter. When the priest told him to open the letter, he knew that it must be something serious. He was reluctant to open the letter thinking that it might be another posting to another parish. He felt sorry for the all the new parishioners that joined his parish. Even though he is flexible when it comes to moving to unfamiliar places, he loved his parish, and he was not ready to leave them right now.

He thought about many things, he thought about starting to learn a new place and people. Finally, he remembered the sufferings of Jesus and all the saints. He remembered that these saints are never tired in their missionary work of saving souls. He surrendered and convinced himself that God has been helping him and the same God will help him overcome and conquer this present hurdle. Looking at the worried look in the senior priest's face he remembered that he may have wasted time meditating and deliberating in his mind, he opened the letter immediately.

He started reading the letter but dropped it immediately on the floor as if something had bitten him in his hands. He stood up and sat down, he squeezed his hands, sat, and came close to the priest and asked him "how can this be possible? How? What? Who did this? Why? As he was asking these questions, tears ran down his face. Looking at his expressions and his face, the senior priest did not utter a word. He was speechless and worried. Fr. Edward cried profusely like a child. The senior priest opened his mouth to talk but could not utter a word. He raised his hands to pat his back but weakly dropped his hands.

After a while, the senior priest simply stood up, went to the restroom, and got some paper towels and offered them to Fr. Edward who gently took it from the priest, mumbled thank you and told the priest that he would like to visit the chapel. When Fr. Edward arrived in his present parish, he furnished the chapel, decorated it in a way that you feel the presence of God. He likes to retreat for quiet time in this chapel. In the middle of the confusion, he went to the chapel to tell his bosom friend Jesus how he feels. He wanted to scream and talk but the only person he wants to talk to is Jesus and Mary. The senior priest nodded in affirmation and then picked the letter still resting on the ground.

Fr. Edward went to the chapel, gazed intently to Jesus hanging on the cross and asked him "Lord, how did you allow this to happen? What have I done? Have I not been serving you well? What will I do? "Serve him" Fr. Edward turned to see who said that. It was the senior priest holding the letter in his hands. He said again "serve him Edward" but how? screamed Fr. Edward, I do not know what to do or how to do it, he continued. The senior priest pointing at the tabernacle, said "ask him, he will help you, he has been helping you" immediately as he said that Fr. Edward looked at Jesus hanging on the cross and the flash of his childhood memories till present came to his mind. He remembered that the senior priest was right. God has been there for him, he has never abandoned him, he knows everything, and he will surely help him do it.

Fr. Edward instinctively stood up and hugged the senior priest, cried again, then suddenly cleaned his eyes, thanked the senior priest, and exposed the Blessed Sacrament for Adoration. He stayed in the chapel for a long time, discussing and praising God for everything that come his way. He remembered that the senior priest was still waiting for him. He concluded his prayers and he felt better than he was before. He had a lengthy conversation with the senior priest.

The senior priest explained what happened, he reminded Fr. Edward that the bishop has been seriously sick which made him to have an unplanned resignation because of his sickness. He was supposed to retire the next year but decided to resign now considering his deteriorating health issues. The senior priest said that the bishop prayed about it and considering Fr. Edward's maturity and trustworthiness, recommended him to be the new bishop of the diocese, and after the due process, the Pope approved it. Fr. Edward found it difficult to believe. He kept on looking at the senior priest as if to ask him to continue talking so that he can convince him.

When the senior priest noticed that Fr. Edward is calm, he announced to leave and went back to his place of work. Fr. Edward thanked him and promised to visit the bishop for more details as soon as possible. When the senior priest left, Fr. Edward went back to the chapel to resume his prayers. When he finished his prayers, he went to the kitchen but could not eat because he lost his appetite. He could not answer his calls even his mom Cathy called. Cathy left a message telling him that they are doing well, and they wanted to hear from him. Fr. Edward switched off his phone and continued his meditation in his room.

Fr. Edward later went to visit the bishop who welcomed him warmly. The bishop repeated all that the senior priest mentioned to him when he visited. Fr. Edward told the bishop that he was shocked when he heard the news but after due consultations with God, he has accepted his fate. He also informed the bishop that he was surprised at his trust in him. He promised by the grace of God to do his best. The bishop blessed him, and he left. The senior priest notified the Nuncio that Fr. Edward has accepted to be the new bishop. Before they made the official announcement regarding the appointment of Fr. Edward, he did not mention the news to the parishioners nor his parents.

When the diocese made the official announcement, Edward's parents almost fainted. They had mixed feelings. They are happy, confident, and proud of their son for his new position, however, they worried because they considered their son as still incredibly young to mount such huge responsibility. They knew that Edward would discharge his work well, but they felt the need to intensify their prayers for him to succeed. The parishioners also had mixed feelings, they are happy for his new position because in consideration of his leadership in their parish, they are confident that he will be a great bishop. However, they are not happy that he will leave their parish. They had been hoping that he would stay a longer period in their parish.

The day they celebrated a farewell party for Fr. Edward was remarkable. A lot of parishioners cried. To a point that the sorrow and lamentation became so intense that Fr. Edward could not help but cry with them. The situation was so emotional. A lot of people shared what they learned from Fr. Edward. Fr. Edward was amazed at all the testimonies people shared from what they learned from him. Most importantly, they learned most of the things from the life experience of Fr. Edward. Fr. Edward uses his educative, innovative, childhood experiences that helped him to preach his homily. He loves sharing his spiritual journey to people.

The parishioners presented expensive gifts to Fr. Edward to show their love and gratitude for how he pastured their souls. They appreciated the sacrifices he made for their own good and the progress of their parish. It pained those parishioners that left their previous parish to join Fr. Edward's parish. These parishioners expressed their concern and begged him to always visit their parish. Fr. Edward expressed his gratitude for their generosity and assured them of a better parish priest which the diocese had assigned to their parish. He pleaded with them to cooperate with the newly assigned parish priest. He asked them to always remember him in their prayers.

Fr. Edward finally became the bishop of their diocese. He prayed assiduously for his new position. He knew that with the intercession of our Blessed Mother Mary who will cover him in her mantle, God will be able to help him as usual. The outstanding thing about Fr. Edward was his humility. He showers God all the praises whenever people come to praise him. He always tells them that all the glory belongs to God. Considering the relationship that existed between him and the parishioners he has worked with previously, he planned to visit them occasionally. He prayed and socialized with them. He went to his home parish to celebrate Mass and as usual, when entering the Church, all the childhood memories rushed back. He remembered all that transpired. He remembered the day he was crying and struggling with his parents outside the Church. The day he strongly refused to enter the Church with his parents. The day he made the decision that helped him reach the position of a bishop.

In conclusion

The book Little Edward and the Church is written to create an awareness and offer a reflective mode for critical and deeper knowledge of what happens in our surroundings, especially in the Church. Edward's experience helped a lot of people to have a meaningful and richer love and dedication for God, the people they communicate with and the activities around them. The book presents a learning experience that helped a lot of people who emulated Edward. Edward's example enhanced their own relationships and situations in their various spheres of life.

The creativity of Edward in his childhood history shaped his life and he noticed the rich values that streamed out of those experiences. Edward was determined to use what helped him to help other people. Most intriguing part of the story was that young Edward who did not want to go to Church because it was boring ended up a great person in the Church. Another attractive part of the story was that Edward found interesting activities going on in the Church which he admired and later joined. For instance, altar servers caught his attention and being an altar server was a huge steppingstone in his spiritual journey as a priest and his relations with people. His major method was that if you did not like something or someone, look deep, you will find something that will interest you which you will admire, praise and love in the person or thing. Another interesting part was that it is much better to be positive than negative.

Edward's childhood experiences propelled him to find, admire and praise something good he found in people and those people in turn strengthened and improved in their performance. Edward's policy remains that there is always something good about everyone. The stories in this book are educative and interesting to read especially the story of how Edward's experiences helped a couple that planned to get divorce and the story of a boy of a single mom, and the absence of a dad in his life affected his behavior and, in the end, found love in his teacher who adopted him as his son and married his mom.

Printed in the United States
by Baker & Taylor Publisher Services